Batter Up Billy

Written by
Brian Williams

Illustrated by
Carissa Harris

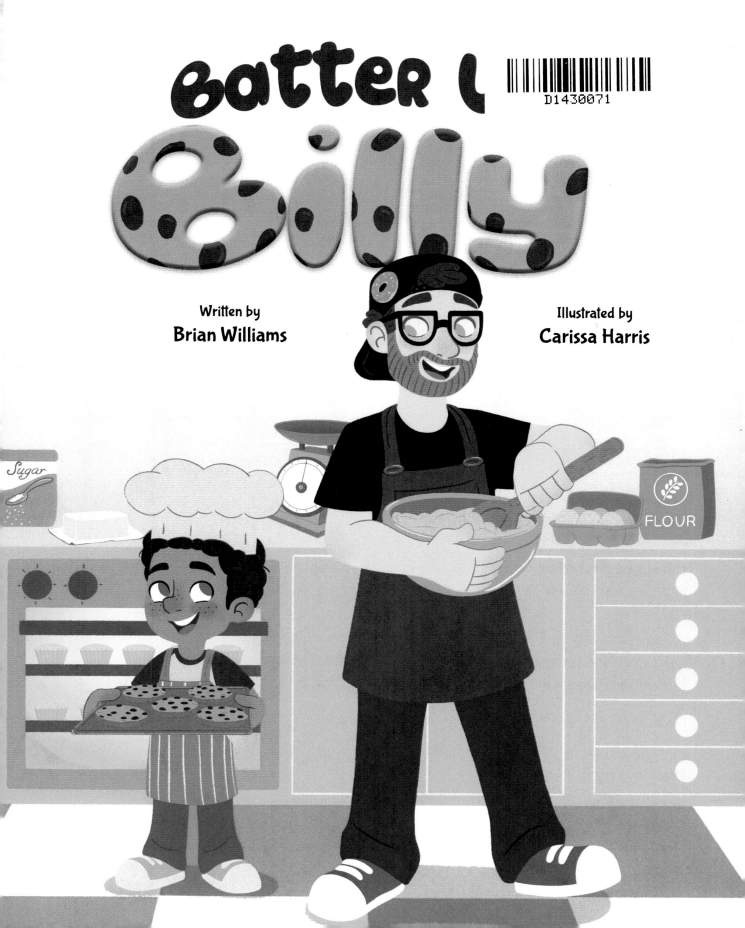

Text and illustrations ©2021 by Brian Williams
Illustrations by Carissa Harris

Photography by ⓘ shootwithjesse

Published by Miriam Laundry Publishing Company
miriamlaundry.com

HC ISBN 978–1–990107–31–3
PB ISBN 978–1–990107–27–6
e–Book ISBN 978–1–990107–28–3

Printed in USA   FIRST EDITION

To all the kids who lick the bowl clean and fill their tummies with delicious batter.

Billy sat at the kitchen table, lost in his Granny's recipe book. Cookies, cakes, and cornbread. The world he dreamed about was hidden in the pages of the torn book stained with food from generations of love.

Cookies
Cakes &
Cornbread

4

"It's time to get to your game," said Billy's dad.

Billy didn't stop reading.

"Billy!!!"

"But Daaaad! This recipe has all my favorites in it," grumbled Billy.

"Now, listen to your father or you will be late for your game," said his mom.

"Fine," Billy mumbled.

Granny winked at Billy as he tucked her recipe book in his bag and dragged himself to the door.

"Don't forget your glove," said his dad.

Billy grabbed it from the corner and headed to the car.

Always last at bat, Billy and his best friend Johnny had other things on their minds. Billy was daydreaming about cake pops, caramel, and cheesecake. Johnny daydreamed about performing in a rock band in front of large crowds.

Billy could almost smell the cake pops when he heard his coach yell.

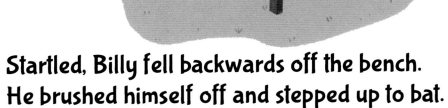

"BATTER UP BILLY!"

Startled, Billy fell backwards off the bench.
He brushed himself off and stepped up to bat.

Ball – Ball – Ball – Ball

Walked by the pitcher, Billy slowly made his way to first base.

To everyone's surprise, Johnny smashed the ball right over Billy's head.

"BILLY! RUN!" shouted his teammates.

Billy ran as fast as he could, but he didn't make it to the next base.

"Out!" declared the umpire.

Head down, kicking the dirt, Billy walked back to the bench.

"Dad ... why do I have to play baseball?" asked Billy at the dinner table.

"Because it's what boys do, son. I played baseball and your Gran Pops played baseball."

"But ... I don't like playing baseball," murmured Billy.

Granny patted his hand.

That night, Billy buried himself in his sheets and had a Big Ole Cry. "If only I could bake cookies and cakes instead of playing baseball," Billy mumbled.

The last tear ran down his face as he drifted off to sleep, dreaming of creating his own recipes.

The next day at school, Miss Becky handed out the science test. Billy started eagerly and confidently answered every question before the bell sounded. Science and math were a breeze.

Recess was the hardest part of Billy's school day.

He was the last to be picked at sports,

the clumsiest runner,

and the shortest basketball player.

Johnny and Billy usually ended up in the corner of the playground, sharing their dreams.

The next day, Granny poked her head into Billy's room. "Is your homework done?"

"Almost, Granny."

"Meet me in the kitchen when you are finished," said Granny with a wink.

Billy raced through his homework and skipped to the kitchen. He found Granny sitting at the table.

"I would like you to make me your favorite cookies," she told him.

"But Granny ... I'm not allowed to touch the oven."

"I will help you, Billy. Now get to your recipe."

Billy knew exactly what to do. He tossed everything he loved from the pantry into a large bowl. Coconut, rice krispies, chocolate chips ....

Soon, Billy's freckles were hidden by all the flour on his face. And, somehow, the floor was covered in butter!

Granny quietly kept an eye on her favorite baker as she knitted away.

Billy arranged his perfectly lopsided cookies on a plate.
"How did I do, Granny?" asked Billy.

"They couldn't be more beautiful," declared Granny.
"Next time, I want you to try cranberries and walnuts.
Those are my favorites."

The next day, Johnny didn't show up to school. Billy struggled all day without his friend, especially at recess.

"Sorry Billy, too slow."

"Sorry Billy, too short."

At the end of a very long day, Miss Becky had an announcement.

"Tomorrow, for career day, we will have a special guest. His name is Baker Beau, and he makes the best cupcakes!"

Billy sprung up in his chair. *Baker Beau!* Billy thought. *A Baker for career day?* Billy's mind was swirling with excitement as he made his way to the bus.

The next afternoon, Miss Becky introduced Baker Beau.

"Who would like to be my special helper?" asked Baker Beau.

Billy shot up like a firecracker and stretched his hand to the ceiling. Baker Beau saw the glimmer in Billy's eyes and called him up to help.

Baker Beau started his presentation. "First, we measure."

Billy's large green eyes were focused on the scale as the weight went up and down.

"We measure carefully so that the ingredients work together properly. Too much flour or too much butter can make our batter too dry or too wet," stated Baker Beau. "Second, we gently stir."

Billy's head moved with every swirl of the spatula.

"We do this to make sure our cupcakes are light and fluffy," Baker Beau explained. "Last, we prepare the batter for the oven."

Johnny raised his hand and asked, "Batter? Like a baseball batter?"

Baker Beau smiled, waited for the class to stop laughing, and described the difference.

After the cupcakes cooled, Baker Beau swirled his spatula as if it was a magic wand. Up, down and all around. Baker Beau continued his magic and, before he knew it, the table was covered with bakery-perfect cupcakes.

At the end of the presentation, Baker Beau plopped a chef's hat on Billy's head and asked him to hand out the cupcakes.

The bell rang and, for the first time, Billy didn't want to go home.

23

That night, Billy found his Mom in the kitchen. "Mom, today I met a baker, and I want to show you that I can be a baker too."

"How do you want to do that, Billy?"

"I want to make you some cookies."

Billy's mom smiled and grabbed the flour, sugar and butter.

"First, you have to be very careful with your ingredients," Billy told his mom.

Billy measured with the precision he learned earlier that day,

stirred the dough with the same gentle technique of Baker Beau,

and carefully prepared the cookie tray as he directed his mom to turn on the oven.

Billy's mom glanced at Granny who was smiling ear to ear.

Billy's mom took the cookie tray out of the oven. The cookies were perfectly round and golden—brown. Billy slipped them onto a plate and presented them to his mom and Granny.

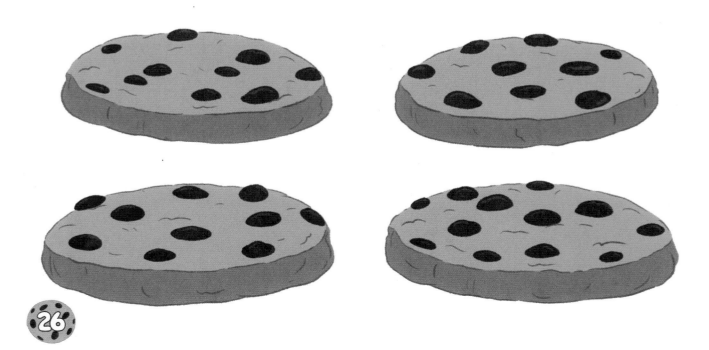

His mom took a big bite. "WOW, Billy!" she said. "These cookies are delicious!"

Billy got goosebumps watching his mom and Granny enjoy the cookies.

The next day at school, there was a new spark in Billy's eyes as he and Johnny sat in their corner of the playground, eating the last of Billy's cookies.

"Johnny, I am going to be a baker when I grow up. If I can be a baker, then you can be a rockstar."

"You mean like this?" Johnny jumped up, slowly put his hands in position, and gave Billy the best air guitar performance of his life.

Just as the bell rang, Johnny gave his final bow.

That weekend was Granny's 80th birthday party. Billy could barely hold back his excitement as it got closer and closer to dessert time. He and his mom had worked hours on Granny's special surprise.

"Happy Birthday to you ... Happy Birthday to you ..." Everyone sang as Billy marched in with Granny's birthday cake.

Granny was mesmerized by the cake. "Billy, those look like cranberries and walnuts!" Granny exclaimed.

"Of course they are, Granny! Those are your favorites!"

"Thank you, my angel. This is the best birthday present ever." She smiled and said, "I got you a present as well."

"You did?" Billy reached into the bag and tossed the tissue paper to the floor.

And there it was ... His very own custom chef hat. Billy's eyes grew bigger and bigger as he read the words on the side ... *Batter Up Billy*. "Thank you, Granny. I'm going to wear it every day!"

Billy and Granny snuggled up on the couch and finished every last crumb on their plates.

Batter Up Billy Cookies

(makes 2 dozen)

Learn how to make Billy's favorite cookies and share them with your friends!

Here's What You Need

½ cup butter (softened)	¾ cup flour	½ cup shredded coconut
½ cup white sugar	½ tsp baking powder	½ cup rice krispies
½ cup brown sugar	½ tsp baking soda	½ cup cornflakes
1 egg	½ tsp salt	½ cup chocolate chips
1 tsp vanilla	1 cup uncooked oats	1 tsp molasses (Granny's secret)

Instructions

Ask an adult before you start

Preheat Oven to 350°F (175°C)

1. Mix the flour, baking powder, baking soda, salt, oats, coconut, rice krispies, and corn flakes in a medium bowl.

2. In a separate large mixing bowl, beat the butter and sugars with an electric mixer.

3. Beat in the egg, vanilla and molasses.

4. Gradually add in the flour mixture until combined. Fold in the chocolate chips.

5. Drop the dough by rounded tablespoons onto a baking sheet lined with parchment paper.

With an adult's help

6. Bake for 10 – 12 minutes or until the cookies start to turn golden brown. Cool on baking sheets for 2 minutes; remove to wire racks to cool completely.

7. Enjoy!

*Create your own recipe by switching out the cornflakes and rice krispies with any of your favorite cereal.